Dear Parent:
Your child's love of reading starts here!

Every child learns to read in a different way and at his or her own speed. Some go back and forth between reading levels and read favorite books again and again. Others read through each level in order. You can help your young reader improve and become more confident by encouraging his or her own interests and abilities. From books your child reads with you to the first books he or she reads alone, there are I Can Read Books for every stage of reading:

SHARED READING
Basic language, word repetition, and whimsical illustrations, ideal for sharing with your emergent reader

BEGINNING READING
Short sentences, familiar words, and simple concepts for children eager to read on their own

READING WITH HELP
Engaging stories, longer sentences, and language play for developing readers

READING ALONE
Complex plots, challenging vocabulary, and high-interest topics for the independent reader

ADVANCED READING
Short paragraphs, chapters, and exciting themes for the perfect bridge to chapter books

I Can Read Books have introduced children to the joy of reading since 1957. Featuring award-winning authors and illustrators and a fabulous cast of beloved characters, I Can Read Books set the standard for beginning readers.

A lifetime of discovery begins with the magical words **"I Can Read!"**

Visit www.icanread.com for information
on enriching your child's reading experience.

Riff Raff the Mouse Pirate
Copyright © 2012 by HarperCollins Publishers
All rights reserved. Manufactured in China. No part of this book may be used or reproduced in any manner whatsoever without written permission except in the case of brief quotations embodied in critical articles and reviews. For information address HarperCollins Children's Books, a division of HarperCollins Publishers, 10 East 53rd Street, New York, NY 10022.
www.icanread.com

Library of Congress catalog card number: 2013951078
ISBN 978-0-06-230508-4 (trade bdg.) — 978-0-06-230507-7 (pbk.)
Typography by Sean Boggs

13 14 15 16 17   SCP   10 9 8 7 6 5 4 3 2 1   ❖   First Edition

Riff Raff

the ouse Pirate

Written by
Susan Schade

Pictures by
Anne Kennedy

HARPER

An Imprint of HarperCollinsPublishers

Down in the rain drain,

Captain Riff Raff

called to his crew.

"All hands on deck!

The *Sea Cat* sails at noon!"

The mice pirates

all lined up on deck.

Cheddar, Munster,

Swiss, and Colby.

But where were Blue and Brie?

Blue and Brie came running.

"We found a map," Blue said.

"Stuck in the grate," Brie said.

"It's a treasure map!"

Captain Riff Raff

spread out the map.

"See," said Blue, "the treasure

is right here . . . oh, dear."

Part of the map was gone!

"All right," said Blue.

"Who's been nibbling

on this map?"

Blue held out her paw.

"Spit it out," she said to Brie.

Brie spit some soggy paper

into Blue's paw.

"It had ketchup on it,"

Brie explained. "Yum."

Blue patched up the map,

but there was still a missing piece.

Which street would lead the pirates

to the treasure?

"Cast off!" said Captain Riff Raff.

"Hoist the *Sea Cat* flag.

We're bound for buried treasure!"

"But Captain," said Blue,

"which street are we looking for?"

"A street that starts

with the letters PLU,"

said the bold pirate captain.

"And the first to spot it

wins a piece of cheese!"

"Out of my way, Munster."

"I was here first, Cheddar!"

Munster drew his sword.

"Take that!"

"*You* take *that*!"

"Pearl Street, ahoy!" called Colby.

"That's not our street," said Blue.

"Pearl starts with the letters PEA,

not PLU."

So they swept along

down the dark, damp tunnels.

"I see it!" Swiss pointed.

"Plant Street.

The cheese is mine!"

"Not so fast," said Blue.

"That's the letters PLA, not PLU."

"PLUM STREET, AHOY!"

called Brie from the bridge.

"I think you're right,"

the captain said.

"It's PLUM, by gum!"

"Yo ho! Yo ho!

A-sailing we will go.

And when we're done,

we'll have some fun.

Yo ho! Yo ho! Yo ho!"

"Thar she blows!" called Colby.

"A whale?" asked Munster.

"Not a whale. A treasure chest."

"Treasure chests don't blow."

"Well, thar she lies, then."

Colby hauled up the treasure chest.

It was set with colored gems.

"Oh, we found it in a

ditch, ditch, ditch!" the crew sang.

"Now we will all be rich, rich, rich!"

Captain Riff Raff turned the key.

The mice crowded around.

He lifted the lid.

They all looked in. . . .

The chest was empty!

It made a whirring sound.

The mice jumped back.

The chest began to sing!

"Oh, we found a magic music box,

here's how we make it sing.

We turn the key and lift the lid,

and it goes ting-a-ling!"